STUCK WITH THE

BLOOZ

CARON LEVIS

Illustrated by JON DAVIS

Harcourt Children's Books
Houghton Mifflin Harcourt
Boston New York 2012

Harcourt Children's Books is an imprint of
Houghton Mifflin Harcourt Publishing Company.

www.hmhbooks.com

The text in this book was set in 23 pt. Aunt Mildred.
The display type was set in Aunt Mildred and hand-lettered by the artist.
The illustrations were painted digitally.

Library of Congress Cataloging-in-Publication Data
Stuck with the Blooz / written by Caron Levis ; illustrated by Jon Davis.
p. cm.
ISBN 978-0-547-74560-2
[1. Sadness—Fiction. 2. Monsters—Fiction.] I. Davis, Jon, ill. II. Title.
PZ7.C579695Stu 2012
[E]—dc23
2011041938

Manufactured in Singapore
TWP 10 9 8 7 6 5 4 3 2 1
4500365076

Special thanks to Adah Megged Nuchi, the best first editor ever. —C.L.

For all the brave investigators of tears
and for Mom and Dad, with thanks for the room to play —C.L.

For Laura and Greta —J.D.

Sunday morning I felt a damp breeze. I heard squishy steps
and a sloshy knock on the door.
And I knew.

The Blooz.

I tried to keep it out.
I shut all the windows,
barricaded the door,
shouted, "Nobody's home!"
But the Blooz oozed in anyway.
It was very big and very wet
and very blue.

"You weren't invited," I said,
stirring chocolate milk for breakfast.
But the Blooz dribbled right into my glass.
"Fine, then I'll make lemonade instead."
But the Blooz squeezed itself into that, too.

"I'm ignoring you!"
I stomped over to my easel.
But the Blooz mixed all of my
paints into muddy colors.

I glared at it. I shook my fists.
"You go away, Blooz, or I'll punch you in the nose!"
The Blooz got bigger and drippier.
It trickled under my shirt, over my shorts,
and into my socks.

"What's up, Blooz?" I asked.

"Did somebody forget your birthday?

Did somebody forget your half birthday?

Is your best purple crayon broken?

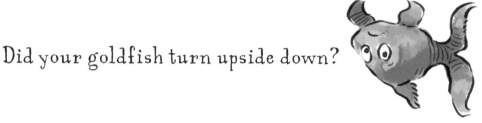

Did your goldfish turn upside down?

Is your sweater itchy?

Do you miss my mom?"

The Blooz didn't answer.

I felt its forehead, rubbed its tummy,
and gave it seven glitter Band-Aids.
But the Blooz was not sick or hurt.

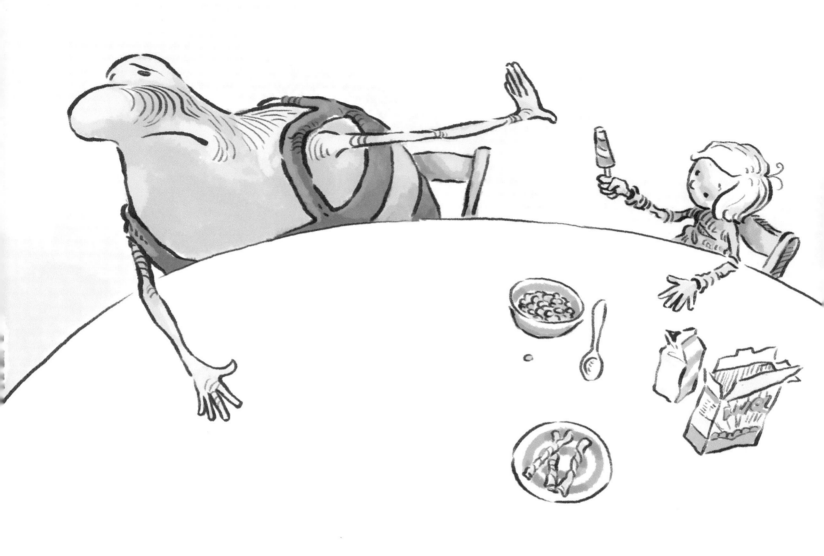

I gave it some cereal, a cheese stick,

and the last peach-raspberry ice pop in the box.

But the Blooz was not hungry.

I brought it my softest blanket, my fluffiest pillow, and even Mr. Croaks.

But the Blooz was not sleepy. It just sat there, large and lumpy.

Empty of guesses, I gave up.

"Well, what do you wanna do, Blooz?" I asked.

It stared a while.

I stared, too.

It slunk into my room. I slunk, too.

We unmade my bed, made a hideout, and hid.

We listened to the house, curled with the cat,

read my favorite book, and made a song out of sighs.

We painted a picture,

turned it into an airplane,

and let it fly.

The Blooz squinted through
the branches. I squinted, too.

We collected only the leaves
with holes in them,

plunked pebbles into puddles,

and kicked dirt into clouds.

I climbed on my bike. The Blooz climbed, too.

We swerved in circles, wobbled down the road,

felt the wind whoosh,

saw the trees whizz,

heard the wheels hum.

It wasn't easy to pedal with the Blooz holding on,

but I used my biggest muscles.

We rode fast, fast, faster.

Zoom, zoom, zooming.

Bounce, bounce—

"Hang on!" I called. **"Bumps!"**

The Blooz held on, till—

Flip! It flopped into the air.
I watched it tumble through the clouds
and fly up to the sun,
high, high, higher.

And then the Blooz was gone.

All that was left was quiet.

And when I looked around . . .

I found the brightest, bluest day.